Pie for Chuck

To Grace, for her
encouragement
and support

I LIKE TO READ is a registered trademark of Holiday House, Inc.

Copyright © 2015 by Pat Schories
All Rights Reserved
HOLIDAY HOUSE is registered in the U.S. Patent and Trademark Office.
Printed and Bound in April 2015 at Tien Wah Press, Johor Bahru, Johor, Malaysia.
The artwork was created with traditional watercolors on cold press watercolor paper.
www.holidayhouse.com
First Edition
1 3 5 7 9 10 8 6 4 2

Library of Congress Cataloging-in-Publication Data
Schories, Pat, author, illustrator.
Pie for Chuck / Pat Schories. — First edition.
pages cm. — (I like to read)
Summary: "Chuck and his woodland friends desperately want a taste of freshly-baked pie,
but they can't get it down from the windowsill"— Provided by publisher.
ISBN 978-0-8234-3392-6 (hardcover)
[1. Forest animals—Fiction. 2. Pies—Fiction.] I. Title.
PZ7.S37645Pie 2015
[E]—dc23
2014039823

ISBN 978-0-8234-3423-7 (paperback)

Pie  for Chuck

by **Pat Schories**

Holiday House / New York

Big Chuck loves pie.

Big Chuck can
see the pie.

Big Chuck can smell the pie.

Big Chuck cannot get the pie.

Can Raccoon get the pie?

No, he cannot!

Can Rabbit get the pie?

No, he cannot!

Can Chip get the pie?

No, he cannot!

Can the mice get the pie?

No, they cannot!

Can the mice get the pie now?

Yes, they can!

Pie for Chuck.

Pie for everyone!

Some More I Like to Read® Books in Paperback

Car Goes Far *by Michael Garland*

Come Back, Ben *by Ann Hassett and John Hassett*

Crow Made a Friend *by Margaret Peot*

Ed and Kip *by Kay Chorao*

Fireman Fred *by Lynn Rowe Reed*

Fix This Mess! *by Tedd Arnold*

Hiding Dinosaurs *by Dan Moynihan*

I Said, "Bed!" *by Bruce Degen*

I Will Try *by Marilyn Janovitz*

Late Nate in a Race *by Emily Arnold McCully*

Look! *by Ted Lewin*

Pie for Chuck *by Pat Schories*

Ping Wants to Play *by Adam Gudeon*

See Me Dig *by Paul Meisel*

Sick Day *by David McPhail*

Snow Joke *by Bruce Degen*

Visit http://www.holidayhouse.com/I-Like-to-Read/
for more about I Like to Read® books, including flash
cards, reproducibles and the complete list of titles.